ODYSSEUS AND THE CYCLOPS

RETOLD AND ILLUSTRATED BY
WARWICK HUTTON

MARGARET K. McELDERRY BOOKS

This book is for
William, Lolly, Jack, and Lydia

Margaret K. McElderry Books
An imprint of Simon & Schuster Children's Publishing Division
1230 Avenue of the Americas
New York, New York 10020

The text of this book is set in Palatino.
The illustrations were rendered in watercolor and pen on paper.
Printed in Singapore
First edition
10 9 8 7 6 5 4 3 2 1
Library of Congress Cataloging-in-Publication Data
Hutton, Warwick.
Odysseus and the Cyclops / retold and illustrated by Warwick Hutton. — 1st ed.
p.   cm.
Summary: A retelling of how Odysseus and his companions outwit the giant one-eyed Cyclops and escape from his cave.
ISBN 0-689-80036-3
1. Odysseus (Greek mythology)   2. Cyclopes (Greek mythology)   [1. Odysseus (Greek mythology)   2. Cyclopes
(Greek mythology)   3. Mythology, Greek.]   I. Homer. Odyssey.   II. Title.
BL820.03H88   1995   398.2'0938—dc20   94-31303

The north wind blew, a wild tempest tossed the sea, one small ship wallowed southward before the storm. Blown far off their true course, the men on board wondered where they would end up.

By morning the gale had subsided. Odysseus and his men, who were returning home from the Trojan War, found themselves on rolling seas, heading toward an unknown island. It rose up before them, green and wooded, abundant with fruit trees and flocks of white sheep. They anchored in a bay. Although everyone wanted to go ashore, Odysseus was cautious. He picked a party of twelve men to go with him, with their weapons and some supplies.

"Why should we need this big jar of wine?" said one man as Odysseus handed it to him.

"I don't know, but something tells me to take it," Odysseus replied.

They moved carefully up from the beach, following a track. It led along the coast and then up into the interior of the island. At length, in the afternoon, they came to a cave with a huge stone on one side. The stone was set like an open door. Inside they found sheep pens, the remains of a fire, cheeses stacked neatly on one side of the cave wall, and vats of sheep's milk.

"This must be the home of a mountain shepherd," said Odysseus. "Let's wait here until he gets back. Perhaps he'll sell us some cheese."

Soon the cave owner arrived. He was a one-eyed Cyclops. A mountain of a man, he towered over the sheep that he drove before him. Odysseus and his men hid at the back of the cave as the Cyclops herded his sheep inside. Then with a thud the great stone door was rolled shut. They were trapped.

Bravely Odysseus stepped forward. "Good sir, we are travelers on our way home. The great god Zeus respects all those who help travelers, and we wonder if you will sell us some of your cheese and let us go on our way?"

"What impudence!" said the Cyclops. "You mean you walked in uninvited and helped yourselves to my home? I am Polyphemus. I don't care a fig about Zeus, and I don't care for travelers. You might be good enough to eat, though," he said more thoughtfully.

The men huddled together in the back of the cave. Polyphemus reached down, with a terrible look in his single eye. He snatched up two men, one in each huge hand, and then . . . he ate them.

Odysseus and his friends trembled with fear and revulsion. After this, Polyphemus calmly swallowed three cheeses, drank some of the sheep's milk, and then lay down to sleep.

In the night Odysseus and his men considered their dreadful predicament. Odysseus wanted to plunge his sword straight into the giant's heart, but he quickly realized that, if he did, he and his men would be trapped forever in the cave, for the stone door was too heavy for them to move. He thought and planned long into the night.

When morning came Polyphemus awoke. With a sudden lunge he grabbed two more men and ate them. Then he milked his ewes carefully and went out of the cave, driving them before him and closing the stone door.

Immediately Odysseus set to work. From a pile of wood
and sticks meant for the fire he chose a long branch. With
his men helping, he trimmed and sharpened it, and then
hid it at the back of the woodpile.

When evening came the stone door was opened, the flock of sheep came in, and the terrifying shape of the Cyclops loomed behind. He pulled the door shut and looked around with his single eye.

"Ah, fresh meat!" he said, reaching down again with his large fists. He ate two more men.

When the giant's hunger seemed satisfied, Odysseus stepped forward. "I would like to present you with a jar of wine. It will wash down your meal."

"What's your name?" asked Polyphemus.

"They call me Nobody," replied Odysseus.

"I'll try your wine, Nobody, and as thanks for it I'll eat you last."

Now the Cyclops had never tasted wine before. The huge and horrifying giant was soon stretched out on the floor of the cave in a deep drunken sleep. Odysseus took the sharpened branch and, with his remaining men helping, he put the sharp end into the fire. Then together they crept up to Polyphemus's snoring head and plunged the red hot point into his horrible eye.

The most terrible cries and groans came from Polyphemus as he staggered upright. From neighboring caves other Cyclopes came running. Through the stone door they shouted, "What's happening? Is someone trying to kill you?"

"It's Nobody! Nobody has gouged out my eye!"

"Well, if nobody is hurting you, you must be having bad dreams," they said and went back to their caves.

Odysseus and his men hid behind the pile of wood as the giant lashed out in blinded fury. Eventually he collapsed, cursing, on the ground. Odysseus waited. Then silently he collected the sheep and tied them together in threes. One large ram he kept separate.

Bitter fury shook the blinded Polyphemus again in the morning. He rose from the ground and, with his horrible hands, searched all over the cave for Odysseus and his men. He could feel his sheep, his cheeses, his milk vats, and the woodpile, but no men, because under each group of sheep one man was hanging.

As the sheep went out through the door he had pushed open, Polyphemus felt carefully again for the men who had blinded him. The sheep trotted onto the sunny hillside. Last of all came the big ram with Odysseus hanging on underneath.

Odysseus and the six men who remained ran down the long path, driving the sheep before them. When at last they reached their friends on the ship, they quickly told their terrible story of the man-eating Cyclops. After the sheep were loaded on board, the ship put hurriedly out to sea.

As they rowed into the bay Odysseus called back to the island, "It wasn't Nobody who tricked you. It was Odysseus of Ithaca!"

When he heard this the blind Polyphemus lifted up a huge rock and hurled it into the sea toward the voice. It raised a tremendous wave just ahead of the ship, carrying it back toward the shore for a moment. The men had to row fiercely to get the ship away safely, but soon a good strong offshore wind filled the sail to drive them home.

That night they had a feast of roast lamb on the foredeck, and the ship plunged on homeward through the night seas.